HEINEMANN GUIDED READERS

INTERMEDIATE LEVEL

GEORGE ELIOT

Silas Marner

Retold by Margaret Tarner

D1005464

HEINEMANN GUIDED READERS

INTERMEDIATE LEVEL

Series Editor: John Milne

The Heinemann Guided Readers provide a choice of enjoyable reading material for learners of English. The Series is published at five levels - Starter, Beginner, Elementary, Intermediate and Upper. At **Intermediate Level**, the control of content and language has the following main features:

Information Control
Information which is vital to the understanding of the story is presented in an easily assimilated manner and is repeated when necessary. Difficult allusion and metaphor are avoided and cultural backgrounds are made explicit.

Structure Control
Most of the structures used in the Readers will be familiar to students who have completed an elementary course of English. Other grammatical features may occur, but their use is made clear through context and reinforcement. This ensures that the reading, as well as being enjoyable, provides a continual learning situation for the students. Sentences are limited in most cases to a maximum of three clauses and within sentences there is a balanced use of adverbial and adjectival phrases. Great care is taken with pronoun reference.

Vocabulary Control
There is a basic vocabulary of approximately 1600 words. Help is given to the students in the form of illustrations, which are closely related to the text.

Glossary
Some difficult words and phrases in this book are important for understanding the story. Some of these words are explained in the story, some are shown in the pictures, and others are marked with a number like this ... ³. Words with a number are explained in the Glossary on page 91.

Contents

A Note About the Author

George Eliot's real name was Mary Ann Evans. She was born on a farm in Warwickshire, England, on 22 November 1819.

Mary Ann was not pretty. In fact she was ugly and wore very plain clothes. But she was very intelligent and well-educated. She learnt French, German, Italian, Greek and Latin as well as English composition and music. She studied religion, literature and philosophy.

As a young woman Mary Ann was very religious. But in 1841 she went with her father to London. In London she met many people and began to talk with them about philosophy and religion. From this time, she said she did not believe in God.

Mary Ann's father died in 1846 and she decided to live in London. In the city she became friends with many famous writers: Charles Dickens, W. M. Thackeray, Lord Tennyson and Charles Darwin. She now called herself Marian Evans.

In 1854, Marian met George Henry Lewes and they fell in love. But they could not get married. George's wife had left him, but he could not get a divorce. Marian and George lived together for 23 years. At first, many people would not speak to them. They could not mix in society. Even Marian's brother, Isaac, did not write to her for 23 years. George Lewes died in 1878 and Marian later married John Cross. But they were only married for eight months. George Eliot died on 22 December 1880.

George Eliot's first story was published in Blackwood's Magazine in 1857. She used the name 'George Eliot' because she didn't want people to know her real name.

People thought that George and Marian should not live

together. They would not have read her stories if they had known that she had written them.

George Eliot was one of the best novelists of the nineteenth century. Her most famous novels are: *Adam Bede* (1859), *The Mill on the Floss* (1860), *Silas Marner* (1861), *Daniel Deronda* (1876), *Romola* (1863) and *Middlemarch* (1872).

A Note About this Story

This story happens in England at the end of the eighteenth and the beginning of the nineteenth century. For hundreds of years, most people had lived in villages and small towns. They had worked on farms and in their own homes. They had never travelled far from where they were born.

But people's lives were changing. Big factories were built in towns and cities. And many people moved to these towns to work in the factories. In *Silas Marner* George Eliot tells us the story of one man's life. But she also tells us the difference between people's lives in a village and in a big town.

PART ONE
(1787)

The People of Lantern Yard

Silas Marner was a weaver[1] who lived in a big town in the north of England. Silas worked hard but he did not earn much money. Six days a week he sat at his loom, weaving linen cloth for his master.

Silas was a gentle young man with a pale face and short-sighted[2], brown eyes. He was twenty-four years old and engaged to be married to a serving-girl[3] called Sarah.

Every Sunday, Silas prayed with the people of Lantern Yard. These men and women were his friends. They met in a small, plain chapel[4] and prayed to God in a simple way. They prayed in this simple way because they believed that this was the best way.

Silas Marner had a strange illness. Sometimes his body became stiff, so that he could not move. He went into a trance[5]. He could hear nothing and even though his eyes were open, he could not see. When Silas came out of a trance, he could remember nothing.

One Sunday, Silas went into a trance while he was praying. The minister of the chapel told the people that the young weaver's illness came from God. When they heard this, the people of Lantern Yard respected[6] Silas.

Silas had a friend called William Dane. But when Silas became engaged to Sarah, William became very jealous[7]. He waited for a chance to harm the young weaver. Very soon, his chance came.

One of the men of Lantern Yard became very ill. He was an old man and everyone knew he was going to die. The young people of Lantern Yard took turns to sit by his bed.

Someone looked after him all the time.

One night, at midnight, Silas took his turn to sit with the old man. William Dane was coming to take Silas's place in two hours' time.

As he sat by the dying man, Silas went into a trance. When he awoke, it was four o'clock in the morning. William Dane had not come. Where was he?

Silas stood up, feeling confused and ill. He looked down at the bed. The old man was dead! Silas ran to the door and called for help. Several people came to the old man's house, but William never arrived. Later, Silas went to work.

That evening, Silas was called to the chapel in Lantern Yard. To his surprise, everybody was there. The small building was full of people and they were all looking at Silas. Some of the people looked sad. But most of their faces were hard and angry.

Silas did not understand. These people were his friends. Why were they angry with him? What had he done?

The minister stood up when he saw Silas. There was a small knife in the minister's hand. He walked slowly towards Silas and spoke in a loud voice.

'Look at this knife, Silas Marner,' the minister said. 'Is it yours?'

'Yes, that is my knife,' the young man answered in surprise. 'I use it to cut the threads of my cloth. Where did you find it? I usually keep it in my pocket.'

The minister frowned[3] and shook his head. 'Where did you leave this knife?' he shouted.

Silas was confused and frightened now.

'I don't know. I thought it was in my pocket,' the young man replied.

9

'Silas Marner, God is listening. Tell the truth!' the minister cried.

Silas did not know what to say.

The minister looked round at all the people. He went on speaking in a terrible voice.

'There was a bag of money in our dead friend's bedroom,' the minister said. 'It was in a locked drawer. The bag has gone and your knife was found near the drawer.

'Silas Marner, you stole that money! You are a thief. Admit these things now and ask God to forgive you!'

For a moment, Silas could not speak. Then he answered, very quietly.

'I know nothing about the money. Search my room. You will not find it there.'

The minister laughed angrily.

'The money was taken in the night. You were in that room all the time. William Dane was ill and could not take your place.'

'Perhaps I went into a trance,' Silas said slowly. 'Someone must have taken the money then. Search me and search my room. God knows I am speaking the truth. You will not find the money.'

A few men left the chapel and went to search Silas's room. The money was not there. But William Dane found an empty money bag in a drawer.

The men returned to the chapel and William Dane held up the bag. He smiled unpleasantly. Everyone sat very still.

Silas looked at the hard, angry faces of his friends.

'I did not take the money,' Silas said quietly. 'I do not know how that bag got into my drawer. God knows I am not a thief.'

Then Silas looked at his friend William Dane.

'I remember now,' Silas told him sadly. 'My knife wasn't in my pocket last night.'

'I do not know what you mean,' said William.

Then other people asked Silas about the knife, but the young weaver would not explain his words. He only repeated in a strong voice, 'God knows I am not a thief.'

The minister sighed[9].

'We are God's people,' he said. 'He will show us the truth. We will draw lots[10], as the Bible tells us. If the lots go against Silas, then he is guilty.'

The minister asked five men to come forward. Then he took out a bag full of wooden counters. Half the counters were black and half were white.

The men prayed. They closed their eyes and, one by one, they took a counter from the bag.

All the counters that the men took from the bag were black. God had spoken. Silas Marner was guilty!

Silas's face went very pale. He looked sadly at William Dane.

'I thought you were my friend,' Silas said quietly to William. 'I lent you my knife and you didn't give it back. You stole the money, not me. You stole the money to harm me.'

Then Silas spoke again and his voice was loud and clear.

'The lots have not shown the truth. God has refused[11] to help me. I cannot believe in Him in any more!'

Everyone gasped in horror.

'Those are evil words!' the minister cried. 'Leave us, Silas Marner. You have no place with God's people!'

Silas said no more. He left the chapel. For many hours, he sat in his room without moving or speaking.

God had spoken. Silas Marner was guilty!

All the next day he worked at his loom. He worked for hour after hour. His thoughts were terrible.

Then Sarah sent Silas a message. She said she was ending their engagement. She was going to marry William Dane.

Silas was completely alone now. He had no friends. God had refused to help him. Silas knew that he could not stay in Lantern Yard.

A few days later, the young weaver left his home. He walked for mile after mile. His thoughts were sad and bitter.

Silas Marner felt that his life was at an end.

PART TWO
(1802 to 1805)

1

The Weaver of Raveloe

The village of Raveloe, in the English Midlands, was sur-
rounded by green hills, woods and fields. It was a pretty
little place, far away from any big town.

Raveloe had a beautiful old church. Opposite the church
was a big, red-brick house. These were the two most important buildings in the village. The old church was the centre of
village life. And the Red House was the home of Squire Cass
and his two sons.

The Squire was respected by all the people of Raveloe. He
owned most of the land around the village and many of the
villagers worked for him.

A little, one-roomed cottage stood outside the village.
Beside the cottage was a stone-pit[12]. No one dug stone from
the pit any more and it was usually full of water.

The little cottage was the home of the village weaver.
The sound of the weaver's loom could be heard every day. It
could even be heard on a Sunday because the weaver never
went to church.

The weaver's name was Silas Marner. Silas had come to
Raveloe fifteen years earlier. No one in the village knew his
sad story.

Unhappiness and years of hard work at his heavy loom
had changed Silas. The weaver was nearly forty years old
now, but he looked much older. His back was bent and his
sad brown eyes were very short-sighted. The village children
were afraid of Silas and called him 'Old Master Marner'.

Silas was a bachelor – he had never married and he had no friends. All day and every day, the villagers could hear the heavy thud of the weaver's loom.

Silas was well-known in the countryside around Raveloe because he walked many miles to sell his cloth. He was a good weaver and he was paid well for his work.

He had no master now and he carefully saved the money he earned. After fifteen years of hard work, he had two leather bags full of gold coins. Silas loved his gold and was afraid of losing it. So he hid the two bags in a secret place under the brick floor of the cottage.

Every night, Silas locked the door. Then he took out the bags and emptied them onto the table. The shining coins poured out. To Silas, the gold seemed alive. The gold coins were his family and his friends. He worked and worked to get more gold.

Silas was not interested in his neighbours and their lives. Day after day, he worked at his loom and spoke to no one. And, as he worked, he thought only of his gold.

But very soon, Silas Marner's life was going to change for a second time. Silas would have to ask for help from the people of Raveloe. Very soon, Silas would have something more valuable than gold. There would be more sadness in his life, but great happiness too.

To Silas, the gold seemed alive.

2

The Two Brothers

It was a dark afternoon in late November. The Squire's two sons, Godfrey and Dunstan Cass, were quarrelling – as usual.

Godfrey was standing in front of the fire. Godfrey was tall, with fair hair and blue eyes. His handsome face was angry as he looked down at his younger brother.

Dunstan was shorter and heavier than Godfrey. Dunstan had been drinking. His face was red and his speech was not clear.

'What do you want from me, Godfrey?' Dunstan said, smiling unpleasantly.

'I want the one hundred pounds that I lent you. The money belongs to Father, not me. I must give it to him.'

'I haven't got it,' Dunstan said.

'What? Have you spent it already?' Godfrey shouted in anger. He raised his hand and walked towards his brother.

Dunstan laughed.

'Don't hit me!' he said. 'If you do, I'll tell Father your secret. If Father knew you were married to a serving-girl and had a child, he'd throw you out of the house. The Squire won't want Molly Farren as a daughter-in-law!

'No, Godfrey,' Dunstan went on. 'You must find the money yourself.'

'I haven't got any money, you know that,' Godfrey said, pale with anger.

'But you've got a good horse,' Dunstan replied. 'Sell

Wildfire – he's worth a hundred and fifty pounds!'

'But he's the best horse I've ever had!' Godfrey cried. 'I can't sell Wildfire!'

Dunstan stood up.

'Then I'll sell him for you,' he said. 'I'll ride him to the hunt[13] tomorrow. I'll find someone to buy him. I've always been lucky, you know that.'

Godfrey turned away and stared at the flames of the fire. He did not know what to say.

Godfrey Cass was a pleasant young man, but he often behaved foolishly[14]. Godfrey had fallen in love with a pretty serving-girl, Molly Farren, and he had married her.

Molly Farren had been pretty, but now she drank and took opium[15]. Squire Cass expected Godfrey to make a good marriage[16]. If the Squire found out that Godfrey had married a serving-girl and had a child, he would never forgive him. Dunstan looked at his brother. He knew what his brother was thinking as he looked at the fire.

'Don't worry, I can keep a secret,' Dunstan said. 'Molly will take too much opium one day and kill herself. Then you'll be free to marry Miss Nancy Lammeter. That will please the Squire.'

'Don't you dare mention[17] Nancy's name!' shouted Godfrey. Then he spoke again, more quietly.

'Very well, take Wildfire to the hunt tomorrow. Try to get a good price for him. But don't drink too much, or you may harm the horse.'

———

Dunstan rode to the hunt early the next morning. He was carrying Godfrey's gold-handled whip[18].

At the end of a narrow lane, Dunstan had to ride past the old stone-pit, near Silas's little cottage. The stone-pit was full of water and the ground around it was very muddy.

Dunstan could hear the thud of the weaver's loom, the only sound in that lonely place. Dunstan remembered the stories that people told about the weaver and his money.

An idea came into the young man's head. Why didn't he and Godfrey visit the weaver? They could make him lend them his money. Old Marner could not refuse to lend money to the Squire's sons! Dunstan smiled. He would sell Godfrey's horse first. Then he would get the weaver's money. He rode on cheerfully.

Dunstan had no trouble in selling his brother's horse to a farmer for a hundred and twenty pounds. Dunstan promised to take the horse to the farmer's stable. But he decided to go on the hunt first. He wanted to ride Wildfire for the last time.

So Dunstan took a drink from his flask[19] and set off. But he was careless. He rode too fast, and the horse fell when it jumped over a hedge. When Dunstan got up, he saw that the horse's neck was broken.

Dunstan himself was not hurt. He took another drink. Why should he care? Wildfire had been Godfrey's horse, not his. He would enjoy giving his brother the bad news. Wildfire was dead and now there would be no money.

There's always Old Marner's money, Dunstan thought. We can have that any time we like.

It was now four o'clock in the afternoon. It was getting dark and mist[20] was all around. Dunstan was not used to walking, but he thought he could find his way home. Holding Godfrey's whip by its gold handle, Dunstan set off.

Dunstan walked along the empty lanes until he was near the stone-pit. The mist was thicker. Then the young man saw a light.

That must be old Marner's cottage, Dunstan thought.

Dunstan was tired of walking. He decided to rest for a time by the weaver's fire. Perhaps the weaver had a lantern[21] that Dunstan could borrow. It was raining now and the muddy ground around the pit was very wet and slippery.

Dunstan walked up to the cottage and knocked at the door. There was no answer. Dunstan knocked again. To his surprise, the door was open.

Inside the cottage the bright fire lit up every corner. The cottage was empty. Dunstan was cold and tired. He walked in and sat down by the fire.

Where is the old fool? Dunstan thought. Perhaps he has gone out and fallen into the stone-pit! And if the old fool is dead, who will get his money? Where is the money?

Dunstan looked around eagerly[22]. He got up and walked about the room. Then Dunstan remembered that country people often hid their money under the floor.

Yes, there, under the loom, were two loose bricks in the floor. He pushed them with the whip. The two bricks moved. Dunstan lifted them carefully and felt in the hole beneath. He smiled as he took out the two leather bags. They were very heavy.

Dunstan stood up, the bags in one hand and the whip in the other. Without stopping to think, he moved quickly to the door and went out. He shut the door behind him.

It was dark now and the rain was falling heavily. It was difficult to walk on the slippery ground, but Dunstan had to hurry. He walked forward into the darkness.

It was difficult to walk on the slippery ground,
but Dunstan had to hurry.

_____

Silas had been to the village. He returned five minutes after Dunstan left the cottage.

The weaver decided to get his money out of the hiding-place. He wanted to look at the gold while he was eating his supper. He went to the loom and bent down to remove the loose bricks.

The hole was empty! Silas's heart gave a great leap. He could not believe that his gold had gone.

With trembling[23] fingers, Silas felt all around the hole. It was completely empty.

Silas stood up slowly. He lit a candle and searched around his little cottage.

The gold was not there.

Silas put his hands to his head and gave a terrible cry. A thief – a thief had taken his gold!

He went to the door and looked out into the darkness. He must find help! Silas began to run towards the village.

The Rainbow Inn was crowded. Suddenly the door opened and Silas Marner ran in.

The landlord[24] looked at Silas's pale face and staring eyes.

'Why, Master Marner!' the landlord cried. 'What's the matter? What are you doing here?'

'I've been robbed!' Silas cried. 'Fetch Squire Cass, the constable[25] – anyone who can help me!'

'Now sit down, Master Marner,' the landlord said. 'You say you've been robbed? How? Tell us what happened.'

Trembling and almost crying, Silas told his story.

'All I want is my money back,' he gasped out at last. 'I don't want the thief punished.'

'How much money was there, Master Marner?' someone asked.

'Two hundred and seventy-two pounds, twelve shillings and sixpence[26],' Silas cried.

'We'll go with you to the constable,' the villagers said. 'That's a lot of money to lose.'

The next morning, all the villagers knew about the robbery. But no one could think who had taken the money.

The rain had washed away all the footprints around the cottage. A stranger had been in the village a few days before. Some people suggested that he was the thief, but the man could not be found.

3

After the Robbery

Dunstan did not return to the Red House, that day or the next. But no one worried about him. Dunstan had stayed away before, sometimes for several weeks.

When Godfrey heard that his horse, Wildfire, 'was dead, he was in despair[27]. Now he must tell the Squire about Wildfire and about the money he had lent to Dunstan. Godfrey was nearly twenty-six years old, but he was still frightened of his father.

Squire Cass was disappointed in his two sons. He thought they were lazy and careless with money. The Squire often lost his temper[28] with them. Squire Cass was a tall, heavy man. He did not dress like a gentleman. But Squire Cass was the richest man in Raveloe. He expected people to obey him and they usually did.

Godfrey decided to speak to his father at breakfast the day after the hunt. The old man was usually in a good temper early in the day. But when Godfrey saw the Squire the next morning he was already in a bad temper.

The Squire stared angrily at Godfrey.

'You're late for breakfast again,' he said. 'You young men are —'

'I've had my breakfast, sir,' Godfrey answered quickly. 'There's something I have to tell you.'

'I'm sure it won't be good news,' the Squire said angrily. 'What is it? I hope you don't want money!'

Godfrey took a deep breath.

'I've had some bad luck,' he began. 'It's Wildfire —'

'What! Has the horse gone lame[29]?' the Squire asked frowning. 'What have you done? I thought you were a good rider.'

'Dunstan was riding him, sir,' Godfrey said quietly.

'Dunstan? You were a fool to let him ride Wildfire. Dunstan is wild and careless.'

Godfrey took another deep breath.

'Dunstan took Wildfire to the hunt,' he said. 'He tried to leap over a hedge. Wildfire fell and was killed.'

The Squire's face went red with anger.

'Where is your brother now?'

'Dunstan didn't come back yesterday,' said Godfrey. 'And I have worse news for you.'

'Then tell me quickly,' the Squire said. 'Go on. What else has happened?'

Godfrey told his father that he had lent Dunstan a hundred pounds of his father's money. Then he told him of Dunstan's plan to sell Wildfire.

'You gave Dunstan a hundred pounds of my money?' the Squire shouted. 'Why, you're as bad as he is!'

The Squire sat and thought for a moment.

'And I know why you gave him money,' he said angrily. 'You've done something wrong and you were paying Dunstan to keep your secret!'

Godfrey did not answer.

'I must have some money,' Squire Cass went on. 'Sell Dunstan's horse and I'll take the money you get for it.

'You two boys behave like fools,' the Squire went on. 'You are both lazy and you spend all my money. Why don't you marry and settle down[30]? Lammeter's daughter would marry

27

you, Godfrey. And I thought you liked the girl. Are you afraid of asking her?'

'I'd rather marry Nancy Lammeter than any other woman,' Godfrey said quietly.

'Then why don't you ask her?' Squire Cass shouted.

But Godfrey could not answer that question.

————

The villagers of Raveloe were kind people. They were all sorry for Silas Marner and did their best to help him.

The kindest of the village women was Dolly Winthrop. One Sunday afternoon, she went with her little boy, Aaron, to visit Silas.

Although it was Sunday, Silas was working. Mrs Winthrop shook her head sadly when she heard the sound of the loom.

'God tells us to rest on Sunday,' she said to herself. 'Master Marner should come to church sometimes. Everyone needs rest and cheerful company.'

Mrs Winthrop knocked on the door gently and Silas let her in.

'I made some cakes yesterday,' Mrs Winthrop said, when she was sitting by the fire. 'They are so good, Master Marner, that I thought you'd like some.'

Mrs Winthrop gave a plate of cakes to Silas and he smiled gently.

Little Aaron, who was seven years old, looked out at Silas from behind his mother's chair.

'It's nearly Christmas, you know, Master Marner,' Dolly Winthrop said. 'You should come to church, Master Marner. You will like the Christmas music.'

Silas smiled sadly and shook his head. When he had lived in Lantern Yard there had been no Christmas music.

'My Aaron can sing like a bird,' Dolly went on, smiling at the child. 'His father's taught him a Christmas carol. Come, Aaron, sing to Master Marner.'

The weaver held out a small cake and Aaron moved nearer to Silas. The little boy took the cake. He would not look at Silas.

'Oh, you've had enough cake, Aaron,' his mother said. 'I'll hold it while you sing.'

Aaron took a deep breath and sang a carol in a high, clear voice.

'That's real Christmas music,' Dolly said. 'Come to church on Christmas Day, Master Marner, and you'll hear more. You should not sit alone at Christmas.'

But on Christmas Day, the snow fell and it was very cold. Silas did not go out of the cottage. He sat sadly by the fire, thinking of his lost gold.

4

New Year's Eve[31]

Christmas came, but Dunstan Cass did not return. Godfrey began to think that the secret of his marriage was safe. He tried to forget Molly Farren and her child.

Squire Cass always gave a big party on New Year's Eve. There was music and dancing and a great deal to eat and drink. People were invited from miles around. The party went on all day and there was room at the Red House for everyone to stay for the night.

Nancy Lammeter and her father will come, Godfrey thought. I can sit beside her. Perhaps she will smile at me. Perhaps we will dance. Perhaps she will let me hold her hand!

Nancy was looking forward to the party, but for a different reason. She was very angry with Godfrey.

Nancy knew that she was pretty and she knew that she was a good match[32] for the Squire's son. In the past, Godfrey had often visited her. But now he stayed away from the Lammeters' house. Nancy was upset and angry. She had decided to look very beautiful at the Squire's party. She would be polite to Godfrey, but she would be very cold towards him. Perhaps she could make the young man speak of love!

And now, at last, it was New Year's Eve. The Squire's guests had all arrived at the Red House. Miss Nancy, Lammeter was wearing a fine new dress. She was the most beautiful girl in the room.

Godfrey danced with Nancy. Then they sat down beside each other. Godfrey looked at Nancy's pretty face and her bright eyes. Godfrey wasn't thinking about his troubles. He began to speak.

'Dancing with you is the greatest pleasure I have ever had,' Godfrey whispered.

Nancy's face went pink. She turned away from him.

'I'm sure that's not true, Godfrey,' Nancy said. 'But if it is true – I don't want to hear it.'

'You're very unkind, Nancy,' Godfrey said. 'If you were kinder to me, I would be a better man.'

Nancy did not reply.

'Perhaps you would like me to go now,' Godfrey added quietly. 'Do you want me to go?'

'Go if you want to,' Nancy answered, looking down.

'I want to stay,' Godfrey replied, smiling.

I'll be happy tonight, at least, Godfrey thought.

––––

At that very moment[33], Godfrey's wife, Molly Farren, was walking slowly towards the village of Raveloe.

Molly knew about the party at the Red House. She had decided that she would go to see her husband on New Year's Eve. Molly was bitter and angry. She wanted to harm Godfrey. She was going to show the Squire and the people of Raveloe that Godfrey had a child.

It was very cold and snow covered the ground. Molly walked to the village of Raveloe with her child in her arms. The child was a pretty little girl, with golden hair and blue eyes, like her father.

More snow started falling and the child was very heavy.

31

Molly stopped and took a small black bottle from her pocket. She held it up.

Yes, she could see there was some liquid left.

The unhappy woman held the bottle to her lips and drank the dangerous drug eagerly.

Molly swayed and almost fell, then she walked on. She was walking more and more slowly now. The child was asleep. And now her mother longed for sleep too.

After a time, the woman fell down onto the soft snow. Her head lay against a small furze bush[34]. She was soon deeply asleep.

At first, she held the child firmly[35] in her arms. Then her arms opened and the child's head fell back. The blue eyes opened wide. With a cry, the child fell onto the cold, icy snow.

Light was shining on the snowy ground. It came from the open door of Silas Marner's cottage. The child laughed and put out her hand to catch the shining light.

Silas had opened the door to watch the falling snow. As he stood there, the weaver had gone into a trance. Silas could not move or speak. His eyes were open, but he could not see or hear.

The little child walked along the path of light. She passed through the open doorway and went towards the bright fire.

The warmth comforted the child. She held out her cold hands towards the bright flames. Then, very gently, she fell asleep.

At that moment, Marner came out of his trance. He shut the door and turned back towards the fire.

Gold! His gold had come back! Silas stared down short-sightedly and put out his hand.

The little child walked along the path of light.

But this gold wasn't hard and round. It was soft and warm.

Silas went down on his knees in front of the fire. Was this a dream? He stared at the sleeping child. He touched her golden hair.

Silas sat down to think. Where had the child come from? Who was she?

There was a cry. The child was awake. Marner bent down and, very gently, lifted the little girl onto his knee.

The child began to cry. Silas held her tenderly[36]. Then he remembered. Crying children were usually hungry. He must give the child something to eat.

Silas heated some porridge[37] and added some sugar. The little girl opened her mouth eagerly. Her blue eyes watched the weaver without fear.

Then Silas saw that the child's boots were wet and uncomfortable. So she had walked through the snow! Silas pulled the boots off gently and dried the child's feet.

Holding the little girl in his arms, Silas opened the door again.

'Mammy! Mammy!' the child cried and held out her arms.

Silas bent down. There were the child's footprints in the snow. He followed the marks to a line of furze bushes. The child cried out again:

'Mammy! Mammy!'

And there lay Molly Farren. Her dark head lay against a furze bush. Her torn, ragged clothes were half-covered with snow. She lay very still.

5

Silas's New Gold

At the Red House the Squire's party was still going on. Godfrey was standing near Nancy. He was full of happiness – the pretty girl was smiling at him.

The big room was very warm now and the door into the hall[38] was wide open.

Godfrey heard a noise and went into the hall. His face went pale. The front door was open and there, in the hall, was his child – in Silas Marner's arms!

Other people had seen the weaver too. Nancy walked into the hall and the Squire followed her.

The Squire had an angry look on his red face. 'Now, Marner, why are you here?' he cried. 'What do you want?'

'They told me the doctor was here,' Silas answered in a trembling voice. 'I need him quickly. I must see the doctor!'

'What do you want the doctor for?' someone asked.

'For a woman,' Silas replied. 'She's dead, I think. Dead or very ill and near my own door.'

When Godfrey heard these words, he was terrified. He knew at once who the woman was.

By now, the doctor had been found. He put on his boots and a heavy coat.

'Is that the woman's child, Master Marner?' the doctor's wife asked. 'Leave her here with me.'

'No, no, I must keep her,' Silas answered quickly. 'The child came to me – I've a right[39] to keep her!'

Silas surprised himself and everyone else by these words.

35

'Now Marner, why are you here?' the Squire cried.
'What do you want?'

The doctor looked at the crowd of people in the hall.

'I'll go to the weaver's cottage. Someone must run to the Winthrops' house and fetch Dolly,' he said. 'She'll be the best person to look after the woman.'

'I'll go,' Godfrey said quickly, putting on his hat and coat.

A short time later, Godfrey and Dolly Winthrop were hurrying along the snowy lanes.

'Why, sir, you are still wearing your dancing-shoes!' Dolly said to Godfrey, when they reached the weaver's cottage. 'You should go back to the Red House at once.'

'No, I'll stay,' Godfrey answered. 'Maybe I can help.'

Godfrey walked up and down in the snow. He could not go into the weaver's cottage because his wife was there. Was she dead or alive? If she was dead, then he could marry Nancy. But if Molly was alive …

At that moment, the doctor came out. He looked at Godfrey and shook his head.

'I could do nothing. The woman's been dead for an hour or more,' the doctor said. 'She's dressed in rags, but she must have been very pretty once. She's wearing a wedding-ring – I wonder where her husband is.

'Dolly will get the poor woman ready to be buried[40],' the doctor went on. 'I don't know why you're here, Godfrey. You're wearing your dancing-shoes too. Come back to the Red House straight away.'

'I … I want to look at her,' Godfrey replied. 'I think I saw a woman like her yesterday. Don't wait for me, doctor.'

Godfrey went quietly into the cottage. He stood for a moment, looking sadly at the dead woman on the bed. He sighed and turned away.

Silas was sitting by the fire, holding the child tenderly in his arms. The child's hair was the same colour as Godfrey's. The little girl looked at Godfrey with her bright blue eyes, but she didn't remember her father. She turned back to the weaver and touched his face gently with her small hand.

'The parish[41] will have to look after the child,' Godfrey said.

'Why?' Silas asked. 'Will the parish take her away from me?'

'You don't want to keep the child, do you?' Godfrey asked. 'You have no wife. What does an old bachelor like you know about children?'

'Her mother's dead and I don't think she's got a father,' Silas replied. 'The child's all alone. And I'm all alone. My money's gone, I don't know where. And now the child has come. I don't understand why she has come. But I'll keep her.'

'Poor little thing,' Godfrey said. He put his hand in his pocket and took out a coin.

'Let me give you something to buy clothes for the child,' the young man said quietly. And, putting the money into the weaver's hand, Godfrey hurried out.

As Godfrey walked back to the Red House, these thoughts went round and round in his head. He was safe now, wasn't he? Molly Farren was dead. Only Dunstan knew about his brother's marriage. If Dunstan returned, Godfrey would pay him to be silent.

No one will ever know that the child is mine. Godfrey thought. I'll give the old weaver money from time to time. Nancy must never know the truth – she might refuse to marry me!

So Godfrey decided to say nothing.

6

The Weaver's Child

The parish arranged for Molly Farren to be buried and Silas Marner refused to give up her child.

The people of Raveloe were very surprised by Marner's decision. How could an old bachelor look after a two-year-old child?

But Silas would not give up the child. He wanted to keep her and look after her. And the kind village women helped him.

The weaver listened carefully to the advice of Dolly Winthrop. Silas showed her the money that Godfrey had given him.

'Can you help me buy some clothes for the child?' Silas asked.

'You don't have to buy any clothes, Master Marner,' Dolly replied. 'I'll give you the baby-clothes that my son, Aaron, wore. They're not new, but they're clean and they'll be very useful.'

So Dolly brought him a small bundle of clothes and showed Silas how to wash the child.

'She's as pretty as an angel[42],' Dolly said as she washed the little girl's golden hair.

'Think of her poor mother, dying in the snow,' Dolly went on. 'But God brought the child to you, Master Marner. The child came through your door like a little starving bird.'

'Yes, it's very strange,' Silas said. 'First my money goes. Then the child comes – to take the place of my money.'

39

'That's true and you were right to keep her,' Dolly said. 'It will be difficult for you at first, but I'll look after the child for you, don't worry.'

'Thank you. You're very kind,' Silas answered slowly. 'I'll be glad if you tell me how to look after the child. But I want to do everything myself. This work's new to me, but I'll learn, I'll learn.'

'Of course you will, Master Marner,' Dolly said gently. 'She's fond of you already. I know she likes you. Look how she holds out her little hands towards you.

'You hold her, Master Marner. You can dress the child. I'll show you what to do.'

Silas took the clothes. He slowly and carefully dressed the child as Dolly showed him.

'Why, you're as gentle as a woman!' Dolly cried. 'But what will you do with her when you're working? Children are often naughty[43]. You'll have to watch her all the time.'

Silas thought for a while.

'I'll tie her to the loom,' he said at last. 'I'll tie her with a long piece of linen. Then she'll be able to move about.'

'Perhaps that will be all right,' Dolly said. 'Little girls are quiet and good. Maybe a little girl won't worry if you tie her up. But boys are difficult. I know. I've got four boys. They would have cried and screamed if I had tied them up.

'I've always wanted a little girl,' Dolly went on. 'I'll teach this little one knitting and sewing[44], when she's big enough.'

'But she'll be my little girl,' Silas said quickly. 'My little girl and nobody else's.'

'That's true. You are her father now,' Dolly answered. 'And you must do what's right, Master Marner. You must bring the child to church, when she's older. But first of all, she must be christened. The child must be given a name in church.'

Silas nodded. 'I want to do what is right for the child,' he said.

'Then you must choose a name for her,' Dolly said.

'My mother's name was Hephzibah[45],' Silas told her. 'And that was my sister's name too.'

'Hephzibah? That's a long, hard name for a little girl!' Dolly said.

'We called my sister Eppie,' Silas went on. 'That's an easy

name, isn't it?'

So the little girl was always known as Eppie. And the golden-haired child brought a great and good change to the weaver's life.

In the past Silas had loved gold. He had worked to get more gold and it had been stolen from him. Now he did not care about gold. He had Eppie. Now he did not work all day and night at his loom. He often left the cottage and walked in the sunshine with Eppie. The little girl taught the weaver to be happy again.

Soon it was summer. Often they walked together through the fields. Everything was bright and new to the child. There were many afternoons when Eppie called 'Dad-dad'[46] away from his work. And Silas was happy to walk in the warm sunshine, pick flowers and listen to the song of the birds.

Eppie was full of mischief. By the time she was three years old, she was often naughty.

'You'll have to smack[47] her sometimes,' Dolly said. 'She must learn what is right and what is wrong, Master Marner.'

But Silas was too gentle to punish Eppie. He could not smack her. And also he was afraid that Eppie would stop loving him.

'Master Marner,' Dolly said one day, 'when Aaron was naughty, I put him in the coal-hole[48]. I only left him there for a minute, of course, but he hated the dirty coal-hole. This punishment was the best way to stop him being naughty.'

7

Naughty Eppie

One summer morning, Silas was very busy. So he tied Eppie to his loom with the long piece of linen.

That day, the weaver was going to make a new piece of cloth on the loom. He needed his scissors to cut the linen threads. Silas was always careful to keep the sharp scissors away from the child. But Eppie liked the sound made by the scissors. Soon Silas began his weaving. Without thinking, he left the scissors on a chair. The weaver's feet began to move the heavy wooden treadles[49]. The shuttle moved from side to side as Silas bent his thin body over the loom. The thud, thud of the treadles stopped Silas hearing any other sound. He was thinking only of his work.

Eppie went to the chair, quiet as a mouse. She picked up the scissors and she cut through the piece of linen. In a moment, the little girl ran through the open door and into the bright sunshine.

Silas went on working. He thought that Eppie was sitting quietly and being good.

But when Silas looked for the scissors, they were not there! And he could not see Eppie anywhere. She had run out of the cottage. Perhaps she had fallen into the stone-pit!

Silas ran out of the cottage, calling Eppie's name.

He went first to the stone-pit, but Eppie was not there. Silas hurried into the field beside the cottage, but the grass was high and Silas couldn't see the child anywhere.

Silas walked across the field. He looked all around, but his short-sighted eyes could only see a short distance.

Then, at last, Silas came to a small pond. Eppie was sitting beside it. She was using one of her boots to collect water and pour it over her feet.

Silas kissed the lost child and carried her home. But then he began to worry about Eppie's naughtiness. The child might run away again. She might be harmed. Something must be done.

'Naughty, naughty Eppie!' Silas said, pointing to the child's dirty feet and clothes. 'Eppie was naughty to cut the cloth with the scissors and run away. Daddy must put Eppie in the coal-hole!'

Silas thought Eppie would cry when she heard these words. But the little girl laughed happily.

So the weaver gently placed the child in his coal-hole and shut the door for a few moments.

There was silence. Then a little voice called, 'Opy, opy[50]!'

Silas opened the door of the coal-hole.

'Now Eppie won't be naughty again,' he said, with a smile. 'The coal-hole is such a dark, dirty place!'

Silas washed the little girl carefully and dressed her in clean clothes. Would Eppie be naughty again? He didn't think so. He would not use the piece of linen again.

The weaver went back to his loom. But when he looked up a few minutes later, Eppie was not there!

Silas stood up. But as he moved towards the door, he heard Eppie's voice.

'Eppie's in de toal-hole!'

And she looked out of the coal-hole at Silas, with her face and clothes all dirty once more!

That was the last time Silas tried to punish Eppie.

*Eppie looked out of the coal-hole at Silas, with her face and
clothes all dirty once more!*

'I can't punish the child,' Silas explained sadly to Dolly. 'She doesn't understand that she's doing wrong. She'll stop being naughty as she gets older.'

'Maybe that's true, Master Marner,' Dolly said. 'You'll just have to watch her carefully.'

So Eppie grew up without punishment. Silas made sure nothing harmed her. And her life with her father was quiet and happy.

When Silas went to sell his linen, he took Eppie with him. The people he visited were always pleased to see them. Everyone loved the golden-haired child. Everyone gave the weaver advice about Eppie and told him he was a good father.

No child was afraid of Silas when Eppie was with him. Everyone saw that Silas loved the child and that the child loved him.

On Sundays, Silas and Eppie went to church. Dolly had said Eppie should go to church, so Silas took her. Then he began to enjoy the music and singing. He enjoyed meeting the people of Raveloe and hearing about their lives. He did not save his money now. He loved the child, not the gold.

Godfrey Cass watched Eppie grow up with the weaver. Sometimes, Godfrey gave Silas money for the child. Godfrey told himself it was good that Eppie lived with the weaver.

Dunstan Cass had never come back. Most people thought he had left England or become a soldier.

Godfrey thought the future was going to be happy. Very soon, he and Nancy Lammeter would be married and have children of their own. Godfrey thought about Eppie too. People would never know that the Squire's son was Eppie's father. But Godfrey would make sure that Eppie had everything she needed.

PART THREE
(1818)

8

Eppie's Garden

It was a bright Sunday in autumn. Sixteen years had passed since Silas Marner had found Eppie – his golden-haired angel.

In the morning the people of Raveloe were coming out of church.

First came Mr and Mrs Cass – Godfrey and Nancy. The old Squire was dead and Dunstan had never returned. Godfrey and Nancy lived alone in the Red House because they had no children.

Silas Marner was walking some way behind Godfrey and Nancy. Although the weaver was only fifty-five, his hair was white and his shoulders were bent. But Silas's brown eyes were gentle and he looked happy. And the weaver was happy because of the young girl by his side.

Eppie was now a pretty girl of eighteen with long golden hair. And there was a young man who also thought Eppie's golden hair was very beautiful. He was walking behind Silas and Eppie as they came out of church.

'I wish we could have a little garden, Father,' Eppie was saying. 'But the ground is hard outside the cottage. I don't think you would be able to dig it.'

'I could do some digging,' Silas answered. 'Why didn't you tell me you wanted a garden, Eppie?'

'I'll help you, Master Marner,' the young man said. He was walking beside Eppie now.

'It'll be easy for me to work in the evenings,' the young

man went on. 'And I can bring you some flowers from Mr Cass's garden. He'll let me bring some, I know.'

'Thank you, Aaron,' Silas answered. 'If you can help with the digging, Eppie will soon have her garden.'

'Then I'll come to your cottage this afternoon,' Aaron Winthrop said quickly. 'We'll mark the ground you want and I'll start work first thing in the morning. You know I'm always happy to help you and Eppie, Master Marner.'

'Oh, Father!' Eppie said. 'We can plant the flowers and do the easy work! I do love flowers, especially the sweet-smelling ones. I'd love some lavender[51] most of all.'

'There's a lot of lavender growing at the Red House,' Aaron said. 'I can get some when I work in the garden there – and anything else you want too.'

'Don't ask for too much,' Silas said. 'Mr Cass has been very good to us, I don't want to ask for anything more.'

'There are always more flowers in the garden than we need,' Aaron replied cheerfully. 'I am sure that I can get some flowers from the Red House.

'I'll see you this afternoon then, Eppie,' the young man went on.

'And bring your mother with you,' Silas said. 'Dolly always gives us good advice.'

When they were alone, Eppie kissed Silas gently.

'Oh Daddy, my little old Daddy! I'm so glad I'm going to have a garden!' Eppie cried. 'I knew Aaron would help us!'

'You're a clever little girl,' Silas said with a happy smile. 'But you mustn't ask Aaron to do too much for you.'

Eppie laughed. 'Oh, Aaron doesn't mind. He likes helping me.'

They had now reached the old cottage by the stone-pit.

As Eppie opened the door, a little dog ran out. A large cat was sitting by the window and a small kitten was playing near the weaver's loom.

There was now some good furniture in the room. It had been sent to Silas from the Red House. There were no beds in this room because two more bedrooms had been built. The little cottage was now pretty and comfortable.

No one in Raveloe thought it was wrong that Mr Cass had helped Silas. The weaver had been a father to an lost child and he had worked hard all his life.

As Silas and Eppie ate their meal, Silas looked at his dear child with love and some sadness. The beautiful child with her golden hair and pale skin was almost a young woman now. Would he lose her one day, as he had lost his gold?

Eppie looked at her father and smiled.

'Now, Daddy, you go outside and sit in the sunshine,' Eppie said. 'I'll clean the cottage before Mrs Winthrop and Aaron come.'

Later, Eppie went to sit outside with Silas.

'Father, that old furze bush must be in our garden,' Eppie said quietly. 'We'll plant it in the corner and I'll plant some flowers under it. We must never forget the place where my dear mother died.'

'Yes, my dear child, we must put the furze bush in our garden,' Silas answered gently. 'We must have a wooden fence around the garden to keep animals out. I'll ask Aaron if he can build a fence.'

Eppie thought for a moment and then clapped her hands.

'Oh, Daddy!' she cried happily. 'There are a lot of big stones near here. We could build them up to make a wall. We could carry the smallest and Aaron could bring the rest.

'Look here, around the stone-pit. There are so many big stones!'

Eppie ran forward to pick up a stone. She stepped back in surprise.

'Oh, Father, come here and look!' Eppie shouted. 'See how the water in the pit has gone down! It was almost full yesterday.'

Silas walked to Eppie's side and looked down into the stone-pit.

'Mr Cass has been draining[52] some fields,' Silas said. 'That is why the pit is almost empty. They are removing the water from the fields. So the water in the stone-pit is draining away as well.'

'How strange it looks,' Eppie said. 'But there are so many stones here, Daddy. See, I can lift this one easily!'

Eppie picked up a big stone. She carried it for a short way, but then had to drop it.

'Take care, child, you'll hurt yourself,' Silas told her with a smile. 'You need someone to do the heavy work for you – and I'm not strong enough.'

Eppie and Silas sat down on the grass. She sat close to him and rested her head on his shoulder.

'Father,' Eppie said quietly, 'if I get married, can I wear my mother's wedding-ring? You've kept the ring all these years.'

'Have you been thinking of getting married, Eppie, my child?' Silas asked.

'Aaron was talking about getting married last week,' Eppie answered. 'He says he'd like to be married. He's twenty-four now and he has plenty of work.'

'And who is Aaron wanting to marry?' Silas asked with a sad smile.

'See how the water in the stone-pit has gone down!'
Eppie shouted. 'It was almost full yesterday.'

'Why me, of course, Daddy!' Eppie laughed.

'Do you want to marry him?' Silas asked.

'Yes, I do,' Eppie answered. 'But I wouldn't want to leave here, Father dear.

'I'm very happy,' Eppie went on, 'but Aaron wants a change. He says that if I love him, I should marry him now. Aaron wants us all to live together – and I do too. Aaron would be like a son to you. That's what he said. You wouldn't need to work, unless you wanted to.'

'My dear child, you're very young to be married,' Silas answered sadly. 'But we'll ask Aaron's mother what she thinks. She always knows the right thing to do.

'I'm getting older,' Silas said quietly. 'One day you'll need someone young and strong to look after you.'

'Then will you let me get married, Father?' Eppie asked in a quiet voice.

'I cannot say no,' Silas answered. 'But we'll ask Mrs Winthrop. She'll know what you and Aaron should do.'

'And here they are, coming now,' Eppie said, standing up. 'Come, Daddy, let's go and meet them!'

9

The Secret of the Stone-pit

That Sunday afternoon, Nancy Cass was sitting quietly in the Red House. Nancy loved her husband, but she was not a happy woman. Silas Marner, the old weaver, had a child to love him, Nancy and Godfrey did not. Their only child had died when it was a baby.

Godfrey had wanted to adopt[53] a child, but Nancy had never agreed.

'It would be wrong to have a stranger's child in the house,' she always replied.

'Then shall we adopt the weaver's child?' Godfrey had asked many times. But Nancy had always refused.

As Nancy sat alone, she thought sadly about her marriage. She and Godfrey were happy together, but Nancy knew that her husband wanted children very much.

Nancy sighed and walked towards the window. It was late afternoon. Soon Godfrey would be home from walking around his fields.

At that moment, the door opened. Nancy turned with a smile.

'Ah, Godfrey, it's you,' she said. 'I was beginning to worry about …'

Then she saw that her husband's face was very pale.

'Godfrey, what's the matter?' Nancy asked in a trembling voice.

'You must sit down, Nancy,' Godfrey answered.

'I have had a great shock[54],' Godfrey went on. 'But I'm

'Godfrey, what's the matter?' Nancy asked in a
trembling voice.

afraid it'll be a greater shock to you.'

Nancy sat down and looked at her husband's face.

'Tell me,' she whispered.

'It's Dunstan, my brother Dunstan,' Godfrey said. 'We've found him – after sixteen years. We've found his body – his bones.'

Godfrey took a deep breath and went on.

'The stone-pit has gone dry – because of the draining. And he has been lying in there for sixteen years. We know it's Dunstan – we found his watch and my gold-handled whip.'

'Do you think Dunstan drowned[55] himself?' Nancy asked quietly.

'No, I think that he fell into the pit,' Godfrey answered. 'And there's something else. Dunstan was the man who robbed Silas Marner.'

'Oh, Godfrey!' Nancy cried.

'The money was in the pit too – all the weaver's gold,' Godfrey said. 'They've taken the ... the bones and the money to the Rainbow Inn. But I came here straight away, to tell you.'

Nancy said nothing. She knew that Godfrey had something else to tell her.

Godfrey looked at his wife and spoke again.

'Nothing can be a secret for ever,' Godfrey said slowly. 'I've had a secret for sixteen years, Nancy. I must tell you about it now. I don't want anybody else to tell you. And I don't want you to find out after I've died.

'When we were married, I was hiding something from you,' Godfrey said. 'That poor woman Marner found in the snow – Eppie's mother – she ... she was my wife. Eppie is my child.'

Nancy looked down at her hands. She sat very still.

'I should have told you before we were married,' Godfrey whispered. 'But I was afraid of losing you.'

Nancy looked up again. She answered her husband sadly. 'Godfrey, you should have told me about Eppie and her mother many years ago,' Nancy said. 'I would have adopted the child if I'd known she was yours.

'Oh, Godfrey! Why didn't we take her when she was a baby? She would have loved me as if I was her mother. I was so unhappy when my own baby died …'

Nancy could say no more. She began to cry.

'I made a terrible mistake, Nancy,' Godfrey said. 'I've done great harm to you and the child. But we'll take Eppie now. I'll be honest for the rest of my life.'

'Yes, Godfrey,' Nancy said firmly. 'You are her father. It's right that we should have Eppie here. We'll give her everything she needs. I'll love her like my own child. And I hope she will come to love me.'

Godfrey smiled.

'Then we'll go to Marner's house tonight,' he said.

10

Eppie Makes Her Choice

It was evening now. Two people were sitting in the cottage by the stone-pit.

Silas was in his chair, looking across at Eppie. The girl was sitting opposite him. Eppie held Silas's hands. On the table near them lay the weaver's gold.

Everyone in the village now knew about the weaver's gold and about Dunstan's bones in the stone-pit.

'I used to love that gold. I counted the coins every night,' Silas said. 'And then you came and I loved you, my child. I loved you very much.'

'I know, Father,' Eppie said. 'I was all alone. You loved me and took care of me.'

Silas smiled.

'You were sent to save me, Eppie my child,' the weaver said. 'I cared only for gold. So it was taken away. And now the gold has come back, and it can help you. Life is wonderful, wonderful. What would I do if you were taken from me?'

At that moment, there was a knock on the door. Eppie ran quickly to open it.

The girl was surprised when she saw Mr and Mrs Cass. She curtsied[56] and held the door wide open.

Mr and Mrs Cass sat down. Then Eppie went over to Silas and stood behind him, facing their visitors.

Godfrey began to speak, slowly and quietly.

'Marner,' he said, 'you're not a young man. You can't do so much weaving now. So I'm pleased that you have your gold again. But you will spend it quickly because there are two of you.'

'We'll have enough, Eppie and me,' Silas answered. 'And we have a comfortable home, thanks to you, sir.'

'But we don't have a garden, Father,' Eppie whispered.

'You love gardens, do you, my dear?' Nancy said kindly. 'So do I. I spend a lot of time in my garden.'

'Ah, yes,' Godfrey said, 'there's a fine garden at the Red House.' He stopped speaking for a moment and then went on again.

'My brother did you great harm, Marner. And there is something else I must say to you.

'You've been like a father to Eppie for sixteen years,' Godfrey went on. 'I'm sure you want her to be happy in the future. Eppie's life is hard here. If we cared for her at the Red House, her life would be easier.'

Silas was confused by Godfrey's words.

'I don't understand you, sir,' Silas said slowly.

'I'll speak more clearly,' Godfrey said. 'As you know, Mrs Cass and I have no children. We would like a daughter in the Red House. In fact, we want to take Eppie – to adopt her as our own child. You'd like that, Marner, I'm sure.

'Of course, Eppie can often come and visit you. And we will make sure that your life here is comfortable.'

Eppie put her hand on Silas's shoulder. He was trembling.

For a long time, the old weaver said nothing. Then, very quietly, he said, 'Eppie, my child, speak. I won't stop you leaving. Thank Mr and Mrs Cass.'

Eppie took a step forward. She curtsied first to Nancy and then to Godfrey Cass.

'Thank you, ma'am[57]. Thank you, sir,' she said. 'But I can't

59

'Thank you, ma'am. Thank you, sir,' Eppie said.
'But I can't leave my father.'

leave my father. And I don't want to be a rich lady. I can't leave the people I know and love.'

Eppie moved back quickly to her father. Silas put out his hand to hold hers.

Godfrey had not expected this answer.

'You don't understand, Eppie,' he said. 'I have a right to ask you to live with us. Eppie is my child, Marner, my own child. Her mother was my wife. My right to Eppie is stronger than yours.'

Eppie started trembling. Her face went very pale.

'Why didn't you tell me sixteen years ago, sir?' the weaver asked bitterly. 'Why didn't you take Eppie then, before I started to love her?

'If you take Eppie from me now, you will take the heart from my body!' Silas cried. 'God gave Eppie to me when you turned away from her. You've no right to take her now!'

'I was wrong, Marner, I know,' Godfrey said quietly. 'I made a mistake then and I am sorry.'

'I'm glad to hear it, sir,' Marner said. 'But you can't change the feelings Eppie and I have for each other. The child's called me father ever since she could speak!'

'But think about what I am saying, Marner,' Godfrey said. 'Eppie will be near you. Her love for you will be the same.'

'The same?' Silas repeated bitterly. 'No, no. That's not possible. We need each other. We've been like one person, these past sixteen years. You'd cut us in two.'

'Now, listen, Marner,' Godfrey said coldly. 'You say you love Eppie. But you're not thinking about her future. Her life could be better, much better. I must take care of my own daughter.' Silas had no answer. What could he say? He did not want to harm Eppie. He loved her too much.

'Speak to the child,' the weaver said at last. 'Do what you think is best for her.'

Nancy smiled at Eppie.

'My dear, you'll give me great joy,' she said to Eppie. 'We'll be so happy with our new daughter.'

Eppie held the weaver's hand more firmly. She stood very still as she spoke.

'Thank you, ma'am. And thank you, sir, for your kindness,' she said. 'But I would never be happy away from my father. He had nobody in the world before I came to him. And he'd have nobody if I left. My father's taken care of me and loved me since I was little. No one can part us now.'

'But you must be sure, Eppie,' Silas said very quietly. 'You must never be sorry that you've chosen to stay with me.'

'I shall never be sorry for staying with you, Father,' Eppie replied. She spoke clearly, but there were tears in her eyes.

'I have never lived in a big house,' Eppie went on. 'I have always lived in a village with working-people and I like the way they live.'

Eppie was crying now.

'I've promised to marry a working man,' she said. 'He'll live here with Father and help me take care of him.'

Godfrey looked at Nancy. 'Let's go,' he said.

Nancy stood up.

'We won't say any more about this,' she said. 'We wish you good luck, Eppie – and you too, Marner.'

And Nancy followed Godfrey, who had turned and left the cottage without a word.

———

Nancy and Godfrey walked home without speaking to each

other. Then Godfrey turned to look at Nancy and took hold of her hand.

'That's finished,' he said.

Nancy kissed him.

'Yes. We'll never be able to make her our daughter. We can't make her come to live with us.'

'You are right. It is too late now,' Godfrey replied sadly. 'I didn't want a child when I was young. And now I cannot have a child at all.'

'So you won't tell people that Eppie is your daughter?' Nancy asked.

'No. I will not,' Godfrey said. 'I won't try to change her life again. But I'll help her if I can.

'I think she's engaged to Aaron Winthrop,' Godfrey went on.

'He's a hard-working young man,' Nancy said.

Godfrey sighed.

'Eppie's a pretty girl, isn't she, Nancy?' he said. 'But she dislikes me, I know that. She thinks I harmed her mother, as well as herself. I've been a fool. I should have married you earlier. And these troubles would not have come.'

Nancy said nothing.

Then, more tenderly, Godfrey spoke again.

'But I did marry you, Nancy,' he said, 'and I am happy that I did.'

'I am glad that I married you, Godfrey,' Nancy answered gently. 'I can be happy and I'll try to make you happy too.'

11

Return to Lantern Yard

The next morning, Silas and Eppie had some breakfast together as usual. When the meal was finished, Silas spoke quietly.

'Eppie,' he said. 'There's something I want to talk to you about.'

Eppie sat down and looked at Silas with a smile.

'What do you want to tell me, Daddy?' she asked gently.

'I must go on a journey and I want you to come with me,' Silas replied.

'Where to?' Eppie asked in surprise.

'To the town I came from – to see Lantern Yard,' Silas said. 'I told you why I left Lantern Yard many years ago. Now I want to speak to the minister of the chapel again. I want to know if he ever discovered the truth about the stolen money. I want to tell him how happy I am now.'

'Oh, yes, Daddy! Let's go tomorrow!' Eppie said. 'Aaron's mother will look after the cottage for us. And I shall have so much to tell Aaron when we come back!'

———

Four days later, Silas and Eppie were walking along the dirty streets of the great northern town. It was thirty years since Silas had been to the town where he was born. In that time there had been many changes. The streets were crowded with people who looked tired and ill. Thick, black smoke from large factories filled the air.

'Oh, what a dark, ugly place!' Eppie said. 'See how the smoke and tall buildings hide the sky! Is Lantern Yard near here, Father?'

'My dear child, I don't know,' Silas answered slowly. 'Everything looks so different now. I'll ask the way to Prison Street. I'm sure I can find my way from there.'

Silas had to ask the way several times before they found the prison.

'Ah, the streets haven't changed near the prison,' Silas said. 'We must take the third turning on the left.'

The crowded, dirty streets were narrower here.

'Oh, Daddy, I can't breathe,' Eppie said. 'How can people live here, away from light and air? How pretty the stone-pit will look when we get back!'

They walked around another corner. Silas stopped. There was a look of shock and surprise on his face. They were standing in front of the gates of a big factory.

'Father, what's the matter?' Eppie whispered.

'It's gone! Lantern Yard's gone, child!' Silas answered. 'Everything's been pulled down and this factory has been built in its place!'

Silas spoke to many people, but no one remembered Lantern Yard. No one remembered William Dane – the man who had called Silas a thief.

When he was in Raveloe again, Silas talked about his feelings to Dolly Winthrop.

'Lantern Yard has gone and I won't think of it again,' Silas told her quietly. 'My home is here now. I shall never find out the truth. Harm was done to me a long time ago, but good has come of it.'

'Oh, what a dark, ugly place,' Eppie said. 'Is Lantern Yard
near here, Father?'

'That's true, Master Marner,' Dolly answered with a smile. Silas nodded.

'It was a dark time for me when I first came to Raveloe,' he said. 'But when Eppie came, the darkness turned to light. And now she says she'll never leave me. That's enough happiness for any man!'

12

A Village Wedding

Everyone in Raveloe thought that spring was the best time for a wedding.

The trees in the village gardens were covered with yellow and purple flowers. The sun shone.

Eppie's dress was white cotton with tiny pink flowers. Nancy Cass had bought it for her.

As Eppie walked out of the church, she looked like a beautiful flower. She was holding her husband's arm with one hand. With the other, she held onto her father's hand. Mr and Mrs Winthrop walked behind them.

Some of the wedding guests were waiting in front of the Rainbow Inn. Later, there was going to be a big feast for everyone in the village. Mr Godfrey Cass was paying for everything.

Aaron, Eppie and their parents passed the inn on their way to the weaver's cottage. Everyone outside the inn cheered.

Eppie had a big garden now. The cottage was bigger too because Mr Cass had paid for more rooms to be built.

The garden, which was full of spring flowers, had stone walls on two sides. In front of the cottage was a fence, through which the flowers could be clearly seen.

'Oh, Father!' Eppie said. 'What a pretty house we have! Nobody could be happier than we are!'

Everyone outside the inn cheered.

Points for Understanding

Part One

1 What is Silas Marner's job?
2 Silas has a strange illness. What happens to him when he is ill?
3 Why is Silas called to the chapel in Lantern Yard?
4 'The lots have not shown the truth. God has refused to help me,' said Silas. What has happened?
5 Who is Sarah? What message does she send to Silas?

Part Two

1

1 Which are the two most important buildings in Raveloe?
2 Where does Silas Marner live? What is next to his cottage?
3 How old is Silas now?
4 Silas has two leather bags of gold coins. Where does he keep them?

2

1 Describe Squire Cass's two sons.
2 Godfrey has lent something to Dunstan. What is it? Why does he want it back?
3 What is Godfrey's secret?
4 Dunstan has a plan. What is it?
5 What goes wrong with Dunstan's plan?
6 What does Dunstan do when he goes into Silas's cottage?
7 How does Silas feel when he comes back to the cottage that night? What does he do?

3

1 The next morning Godfrey tells his father some bad news. What is this news?
2 Who does Squire Cass think Godfrey should marry?
3 Who goes to visit Silas?

4

1 Why is Nancy Lammeter looking forward to the party at the Red House?
2 Why is Molly Farren going to the Red House?
3 Why doesn't she reach the Red House?
4 Why doesn't Silas see Molly's little girl go into his cottage?
5 Why does Silas believe his gold has come back?
6 What does Silas discover when he follows the footprints in the snow?

5

1 Why is Godfrey terrified when Silas comes into the hall of the Red House?
2 Godfrey walks up and down in the snow outside the weaver's cottage. What is he thinking about?
3 What does Silas want to do with the child?
4 What does Godfrey decide to do?

6

1 What help does Dolly Winthrop give to Silas?
2 'What will you do with her when you're working?' Dolly asks Silas. What is his answer?
3 Why does Silas call the child Eppie?
4 How does Eppie change Silas's life?
5 What did Dolly do with Aaron when he was naughty?

7

1 Silas ties Eppie to his loom. How does she escape?
2 Silas puts Eppie in the coal-hole. Does this teach her not to be naughty?
3 How does Godfrey show that he hasn't forgotten Eppie?
4 Why does Godfrey think that the future is going to be happy?

Part Three

8

1 How old are Silas and Eppie now?
2 Who is going to help Eppie make a garden?
3 How has Silas's cottage changed?
4 Why does Eppie want to plant the furze bush in her garden?
5 What is happening to the stone-pit?
6 Eppie tells Silas that Aaron wants to marry her. What does Silas say?

9

1 Godfrey wants to adopt a child. Why? What does Nancy want to do?
2 Godfrey comes back from his walk. What does he tell Nancy?
3 Godfrey tells Nancy a secret. What is this secret?
4 What do Godfrey and Nancy decide to do?

10

1 What has been given back to Silas Marner? How does Silas feel about this?
2 Godfrey tells Silas and Eppie that he wants to adopt Eppie. What is Eppie's answer?
3 Godfrey tells Silas and Eppie that he is Eppie's father. How does Silas feel?
4 Nancy and Godfrey leave Silas's cottage. How does Godfrey feel about his past mistakes now?

11

1 Why does Silas want to return to Lantern Yard?
2 What does Silas find out when he gets to the town he came from?
3 What does Eppie see in the great northern town?

12

1 Whose wedding is this?
2 Who has paid for this wedding?
3 Why is Eppie happy?

Glossary

1 **weaver** (page 8)
   someone who makes cloth. A weaver uses a machine called a *loom*. On a loom, long threads are fastened to a wooden frame. The weaver pushes *treadles* with his feet to raise and lower the threads. He has a *shuttle* which carries more thread. He moves the shuttle with his hands from side to side between the long threads to fasten them together into cloth.
   At this time, most weaving was done by weavers, like Silas Marner. But very soon, most of the weaving was done by machines in big factories.

2 **short-sighted** (page 8)
   not able to see things very well because there is something wrong with your eyes.

3 **serving-girl** (page 8)
   a young woman who works as a servant in someone's house.

4 **chapel** (page 8)
   the Christian church where the people of Lantern Yard pray to God. All the people who live in Lantern Yard believe in worshipping God in the same way, so they have a chapel which is just for them.

5 **trance** (page 8)
   when Silas *goes into a trance*, he behaves as if he is asleep. His eyes are open but he cannot see or hear anything. When he *comes out of a trance* he behaves in a normal way again.

6 **respected** – *to respect* (page 8)
   think well of someone because they are clever and important.

7 **jealous** (page 8)
   disliking someone and feeling angry with them because they have something you want.

8 **frowned** (page 9)
   when someone frowns they pull their eyebrows towards each other because they are angry.

9 **sighed** – *to sigh* (page 11)
   breathe loudly to show you are disappointed, angry or sad.

10 **lots** – *draw lots* (page 11)
   people draw lots as a way of deciding something. In this story the people of Lantern Yard believe that God will show them the truth

about the stolen money if they draw lots. Five men close their eyes and each man takes a wooden counter from a bag. There are white counters and black counters. If more black counters than white counters are chosen, people will believe Silas is a thief. If more white counters than black counters are chosen, people will believe he is not a thief.

11 *refused* (page 11)
would not do something.

12 *stone-pit* (page 16)
a very large hole in the ground. The hole is there because people have dug stone out of the ground and taken it away to use for building houses etc.

13 *hunt* (page 20)
when people go on a hunt they ride on horseback and chase and kill wild animals as a sport.

14 *foolishly* (page 20)
if you behave foolishly, you behave stupidly, not in an intelligent or thoughtful way.

15 *opium* (page 20)
a drug made from the seeds of a poppy flower.

16 *marriage* – *make a good marriage* (page 20)
Squire Cass expects Godfrey will marry a woman whose family has plenty of money.

17 *mention* – *dare mention* (page 20)
if you say 'Don't you dare ...' you are showing that you are angry. Godfrey is angrily telling his brother not to talk about Nancy.

18 *whip* (page 20)
a long piece of leather fastened to a handle. It is used for hitting a horse to make it move faster.

19 *flask* (page 21)
a small, flat bottle you can put in your pocket. Flasks often contain alcohol.

20 *mist* (page 21)
a cloud of small drops of water in the air close to the ground. It is difficult to see if there is mist.

21 *lantern* (page 22)
a lamp, made from metal and glass, that you can carry with you. Light comes from the flame of a candle or from burning oil inside the lantern.

22 *eagerly* (page 22)

wanting something very much. Dunstan wants to find Marner's money.

23 *trembling* (page 24)

shaking because you are excited or afraid or very worried.

24 *landlord* (page 24)

the man who owns the inn.

25 *constable* (page 24)

a policeman. In a small village like Raveloe the constable was one of the villagers. He did not work all the time as a policeman.

26 *sixpence – two hundred and seventy-two pounds, twelve shillings and sixpence* (page 25)

pounds, shillings and pence were the coins used in England at this time. This is a very large amount of money for a poor man to have.

27 *despair – was in despair* (page 26)

Godfrey felt that everything had gone wrong and that he could do nothing to makes things better again.

28 *temper – lost his temper* (page 26)

became angry. If you are in a *bad temper* you feel angry. If you are in a *good temper* you feel happy.

29 *lame* (page 27)

unable to walk properly because a leg is hurt.

30 *settle down* (page 27)

start living a quiet life.

31 *New Year's Eve* (page 30)

the 31st of December, the day before the beginning of a new year on 1st January.

32 *match – good match* (page 30)

the right sort of person for Godfrey to marry. See Glossary no. 16.

33 *moment – At that very moment* (page 31)

at exactly the same time.

34 *bush – furze bush* (page 32)

a plant with yellow flowers and sharp green leaves. It is a wild plant and doesn't usually grow in gardens.

35 *firmly* (page 32)

if you hold on to something firmly, you hold it tightly. If you speak firmly, you speak in a way that shows you believe what you say.

36 *tenderly* (page 34)

gently and lovingly.

37 **porridge** (page 34)
oats (corn) cooked in milk or water to make a meal. Porridge is like a thick soup.

38 **hall** (page 35)
the part of a house that you enter after you go through the front door.

39 **right** – *to have a right* (page 35)
be able to do something or to own something for a special and important reason. Silas says he has a right to keep the child because she came into his house.

40 **buried** – *to bury* (page 37)
to bury someone is to put them under the ground after they are dead.

41 **parish** (page 38)
England is divided into counties, and each county is divided into parishes. The officials of a parish had to look after poor people who did not have homes.

42 **angel** (page 39)
in the Christian religion, angels are God's servants in heaven. In pictures, they are usually beautiful and have golden hair.

43 **naughty** (page 41)
children are said to be naughty when they behave badly.

44 **sewing** – *knitting and sewing* (page 41)
sewing is making or mending clothes using a needle and thread. Knitting is making clothes using two big needles and wool.

45 **Hephzibah** (page 41)
pronounced /hepzɪbɑː/

46 **Dad-dad** (page 42)
a child's name for her father.

47 **smack** – *to smack* (page 42)
hit someone with your hand.

48 **coal-hole** (page 42)
the small cupboard next to the fire where coal is kept.

49 **treadles** (page 43)
see Glossary no. 1.

50 **Opy** (page 44)
a child's way of saying 'open'.

51 **lavender** (page 49)
a sweet-smelling plant with small purple flowers.

52 *draining* (page 51)

removing water from somewhere because there is too much of it. A farmer might drain fields so that he can use the fields to grow crops.

53 *adopt* – *to adopt* (page 54)

take someone else's child into your family. The child becomes your son or daughter by law.

54 *shock* (page 54)

an unpleasant surprise.

55 *drowned* – *to drown* (page 56)

die because you fall into water and are not able to breathe.

56 *curtsied* (page 58)

bent her knees and lowered her body towards the ground. Eppie is being polite to Nancy when she curtsies.

57 *ma'am* (page 59)

a short way of saying madam. This is a polite way of speaking to a lady.

INTERMEDIATE LEVEL

Oliver Twist *by Charles Dickens*
The Bonetti Inheritance *by Richard Prescott*
No Comebacks *by Frederick Forsyth*
The Enchanted April *by Elizabeth Von Arnim*
The Three Strangers *by Thomas Hardy*
Shane *by Jack Schaefer*
Old Mali and the Boy *by D.R. Sherman*
Tales of Goha *by Leslie Caplan*
The Smuggler *by Piers Plowright*
The Pearl *by John Steinbeck*
The Woman Who Disappeared *by Philip Prowse*
A Town Like Alice *by Nevil Shute*
The Queen of Death *by John Milne*
Walkabout *by James Vance Marshall*
Meet Me in Istanbul *by Richard Chisholm*
The Great Gatsby *by F. Scott Fitzgerald*
The Space Invaders *by Geoffrey Matthews*
My Cousin Rachel *by Daphne du Maurier*
I'm the King of the Castle *by Susan Hill*
Dracula *by Bram Stoker*
The Speckled Band and Other Stories *by Sir Arthur Conan Doyle*
The Queen of Spades and Other Stories *by Aleksandr Pushkin*
The Diamond Hunters *by Wilbur Smith*
When Rain Clouds Gather *by Bessie Head*
Banker *by Dick Francis*
No Longer at Ease *by Chinua Achebe*
The Franchise Affair *by Josephine Tey*
The Case of the Lonely Lady *by John Milne*

For further infomation on the full selection of
Readers at all five levels in the series, please refer
to the Heineman Guided Readers catalogue.

Heinemann English Language Teaching
A division of Heinemann Publishers (Oxford) Ltd
Halley Court, Jordan Hill, Oxford OX2 8EJ

OXFORD   MADRID   ATHENS   PARIS   FLORENCE   PRAGUE
SÃO PAULO   CHICAGO   MELBOURNE   AUCKLAND
SINGAPORE   TOKYO   IBADAN   GABORONE
JOHANNESBURG   PORTSMOUTH (NH)

ISBN 0 435 27251 9

This retold version for Heinemann Guided Readers
© Margaret Tarner 1994
First published 1994

Illustrated by Anthony Meadows
Typography by Adrian Hodgkins
Designed by Sue Vaudin
Cover by Peter Murphy and Threefold Design
Set in 11/12.5 Goudy
Printed and bound in Malta

94   95   96   97   98   10   9   8   7   6   5   4   3   2   1